This is the true story of what happened to somebody's head while travelling through 28 cities and 15 countries in 31 days, alone. The trip took place in the summer of 1995, and the book was finished in 2008. The book contains notebook entries from the time of the trip, and there are photographs from each of the cities. Some photos are quite nice and some are just plain weird.

Mick MacO is an Irish graphic designer who lives in Germany. He is married with no children and a cat called Samuel Longhorn Clemens. Mick MacO is a shortened version of the author's Gaelic name, which is too long to pronounce.

Mick MacO.

Foreword

The way this book came about is a story in itself. Ever since my trip around Europe I've been writing, and not knowing why I'm writing, or why I want to write or why I need to write. But I've been constantly writing.

It came to a point where I found myself writing lots of little short stories, which just came out without me thinking about it. During this time I found a library book called "Writing with both sides of the brain", and that struck a chord, so I borrowed it and read through it.

Some of the techniques described in the book were 'brainstorming' (or 'mind mapping') and 'rapid writing'. So I tried these techniques and answered the questions and did the exercises. One of them asked, "Why do you write?" You had to answer it using 'rapid writing', i.e. write whatever comes into your head without thinking, for, say, five minutes, and if you can't think of anything to write, you write, "I can't think of anything to write."

I had about three or four points written down and I still had over a minute left to go. Without thinking I wrote, "Well maybe someday I'll write the story of that trip around Europe." The next question in the exercise was "Why don't you do that?" And I didn't have a proper answer to that. So I mentioned it to Mrs. MacO. She said "Why Not?"

ISBN 978-1-84799-434-9

Mick MacO would like to thank all his family and friends,
in particular Ankirella, Derham "Derham" Derham, Cockney Jeff
and Presbo Dave for their support, advice and patience.

www.MickMacO.org

For Mrs. Mac O.

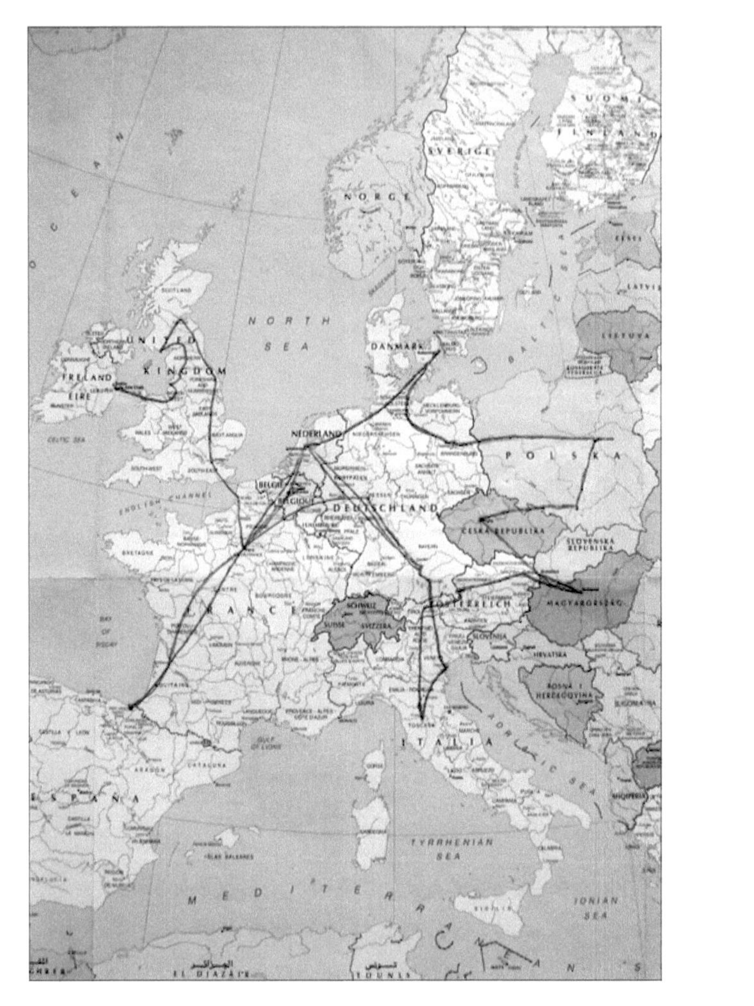
NORTH SEA
UNITED KINGDOM
IRELAND
EIRE
SCOTLAND
CELTIC SEA
ENGLISH CHANNEL
NORGE
SVERIGE
SUOMI
FINLAND
DANMARK
LIETUVA
NEDERLAND
POLSKA
DEUTSCHLAND
ČESKÁ REPUBLIKA
SLOVENSKÁ REPUBLIKA
MAGYARORSZÁG
ÖSTERREICH
SCHWEIZ
SUISSE
SVIZZERA
SLOVENIJA
HRVATSKA
BOSNA I HERCEGOVINA
FRANCE
BRETAGNE
BAY OF BISCAY
ESPAÑA
ARAGON
CATALUNA
GULF OF LIONS
ITALIA
TOSCANA
ADRIATIC SEA
TYRRHENIAN SEA
IONIAN SEA
ILLES BALEARES
MEDITERRANEAN
EL DJAZAÏR
TOUNIS

TRIP

1. Intro – Dublin
2. Amsterdam
3. Copenhagen
4. Berlin
5. Warsaw
6. Krakow
7. Auschwitz
8. Prague
9. Budapest
10. Vienna
11. Innsbruck
12. Florence
13. Venice
14. Bamberg
15. Amsterdam Again
16. Gent
17. Antwerp
18. Brussels
19. Paris
20. San Sebastian
21. Bamberg Again
22. Amsterdam Again II
23. Paris Again
24. London
25. Edinburgh
26. Glasgow
27. Liverpool
28. Holyhead
29. Dun Laoghaire
30. Epilogue

1. Intro - Dublin

Dun Laoghaire is the port town on the south side of Dublin, named after the Gaelic King Laoghaire. Trains run through where his fort once stood. In 1971 I was born in Dun Laoghaire hospital, and grew up to be a fun-loving, out-going, not-as-open-minded-as-I-liked-to-think Dubliner.

On a sunny day in May 1995 I headed off from Dun Laoghaire harbour on the ferry to Holyhead in Wales. This was the start of a summer working in Amsterdam, which would hopefully be topped off with a trip around Europe. It was the fourth year in a row I'd planned to go inter-railing, and this year I was going to do it if it killed me.

In Amsterdam you always had an incredibly fantastic time. Loads of the lads and lasses from Ireland were going over this year, so an amazing time was expected once again. It was all about having experiences that you'd never had before. There was a big old world out there, and inter-railing was one way of checking it out. Other people had done it and had the time of their lives. My inner voice kept telling me that it simply had to be done. I was also single for the first time in half a decade.

Before leaving I'd read *On the Road* by Jack Kerouac, and was foaming at the mouth with the idea of roaming off. I started my travel notebook with an upbeat entry…

...Yes, this summer it's - Europa here we come!
Start up your engines, batten down the hatches,
lock up your daughters, and pull out all the stops!
Living life to the full. And feck the begrudgers..

I'd been having loads of crazy thoughts about what "IT" was that humans didn't know, i.e. the great unknown. I reckoned that the "known" couldn't amount to a hell of a lot compared to "the unknown". Know what I mean?

Anyway, on 14th August I left Amsterdam Central Station on a train headed for Copenhagen. Over the next 31 days I would travel through 28 cities in 15 different countries, alone. This is the story of what happened to my head on the trip.

2. Amsterdam

The ferry pulled out of Dun Laoghaire Harbour and into the open sea. The further the boat got away from land the better I felt. Finally the adventure had started. I was heading off at last to Amsterdam via London. Looking back at little old Ireland the sun was just going down over Howth – so long for now. That night on the boat I watched Ajax Amsterdam win the European Champions League – that had to be a good omen.

The ferry pulled into a dark Holyhead, where I couldn't find a cigarette machine for love nor money. The bus wound its way down through England to London and got there at around 9ish. I passed loads of memories along the way - Regent's Park, Marble Arch, and Oxford Street. I'd lived here four summers before and loved it.

One of the lads from Ireland was staying in London before travelling on to Amsterdam with me. He met me off the bus. We walked and talked back to his place above a pub somewhere in the centre of the city. The following 36 hours in London were amazing. We hung out in Camden and went on the session in Covent Garden and Leicester Square with another friend from Ireland living in London. We ended up singing "I want to break Free" by Queen with a busker outside the Hippodrome. Good buzz.

On the third day we arose, and got a bus down to Dover. Every single person on the boat was weird except for us, or so it seemed. Over we hopped to Calais. The friendly bus driver with the unorthodox haircut drove us through France and Belgium to Holland. We had a good laugh along the way – having sign-language chats with truck drivers as we went.

When we got into Amsterdam we headed straight for the Good Times coffee shop. We sat in the morning sun feeling like the Kings of the Earth. We'd made it. Amsterdam! Let the good times flow...

After a re-acquaintance with the city we headed for the trees. The campsite we were staying in was in a big forest on the edge of Amsterdam called "Het Amsterdamse Bos". It was beautiful, and unlike Ireland where everything was wild, this neck of the woods was all man-made. So it had a very different vibe to it, especially if you smoked really good marijuana. There you have it.

Loads of scruffy immigrants like us lived on the campsite in the summer and worked in the greenhouses outside Amsterdam. It was its own little sub-culture – lots of partying lunatics. We lived in the "Irish field", which was mostly full of Irish (funnily), as well as English, Scottish, and assorted nutty folk. Rarely was there a dull moment, and if ever, not for long.

That summer I ended up doing a load of writing; trying to sort my head out with a pen. Making an effort to figure out what was going on in and out of my mind, with the notebook…

…What a rush of a fucking time I'm having- my head is so free and glad to have so much well, headspace - and there's so many things running around inside in my little mind - like… Could it be that there is some unknown entity that people have interpreted in many ways, but can't understand, and whatever the fuck IT is – we're not supposed to know? You never know…

It was this kind of a head that I was walking around with. After seven weeks of work I had enough Guilders for the trip. I proudly purchased the inter-railing ticket in Central Station.

This year it was finally going to happen! I'd be travelling very light (essentials only: notebook, personal stereo, books, juggling balls, and just enough clothes). I was planning to sleep on the trains most nights in between cities – saving money, but more importantly, time.

3. Copenhagen

Time dragged between buying the ticket and the day of the trip. Finally on Sunday 13th August I set off from Amsterdam. There was a farewell session with the lads and lasses from the campsite in Amsterdam. They ceremoniously saw me off; delighted to be rid of someone who couldn't stop talking about going inter-railing.

In Denmark the train drove onto a boat and then off again. I'd never experienced that before. Arriving in Copenhagen (or 'Kobenhaven' as it's really called) I was full of anticipation. After stashing my bag in a train station locker I explored the vicinity around the train station. My guide book had a little map so you couldn't miss all the main important historical bits. The Copenhagen architecture and the babes were amazing (not in that order). The Danish language was very intriguing – an obvious cousin of Dutch and Deutsch, but with its own unique characters, like "Ø" and "Æ".

The city was amazingly clean, almost freakishly so – especially compared to Amsterdam's rougher parts. I walked around with a festive sensation – "I'm finally on Holiday!" The feeling was just starting to sink in after a summer of greenhouse work.

Having strolled around the center of (wonderful, wonderful) Copenhagen, I just couldn't put it off any longer – it was time to check out Christiania. I'd only recently heard about this place – an apparently lawless independent "state" within Copenhagen. That was pretty much all I knew. But I'd met a few different people who'd suggested seeing it.

It seemed almost impossible that this crazy anarchist place could be beyond what seemed like normal streets. But it was. And it *was* strange. The first indication of anything out of the ordinary was a huge statue made of scrap metal on a corner, like a sinister Statue of Liberty. This didn't fit in with the rest of the city's vibe. Then further down the road was a wooden entrance gate with "Christiania" painted above it. So here I was on the "civilized" side of this mysterious place.

Some dodgy stories about this neighbourhood had circulated in Amsterdam. I didn't quite know what to believe – or expect. Was it a good idea going in here alone? Sod it; I had to check it out. Walking through the gate I thought – this should be interesting either way. I took a deep breath.

Beyond a few bushes and trees I could see some ramshackle buildings and then a semi-circle of stalls selling all sorts of stuff, like at your average rock festival or something. I went over and had a wander around, stopping at one that was selling bongs, pipes and rolling papers. I asked the guy if he spoke English.

"Is that a Dublin accent?" came the reply. The guy's name was Seámus and he was from Clondalkin in Dublin – a turn up for the books, or what? There I was crapping myself about going into this place with no laws and loads of weirdos and the first head I meet is a fellow Dubliner. Classic!

Seámus was sound. He brought me around the back of his stall, poured some coffee and skinned up a joint. He explained that Christiania was pretty much a big hippie commune with a bad name – mostly because the authorities wanted it closed down. They *did* have some trouble with hard drugs, as well as the odd psychopathic lunatic. But basically it was nothing worse than Dublin city centre on an average Saturday night, reckoned Seámus.

"Freetown Christiania" was originally an old barracks that were abandoned. In the sixties some squatters moved in, and before long it was full of various inhabitants. It developed its own independent community with no laws, but a set of "rules": no cars, no stealing, no guns, no hard drugs etc. Voluntary Committees ran the whole thing. Needless to say the powers-that-be weren't pleased about this city within a city. But it had survived and thrived under its own steam. It was without doubt a unique spot, I thought.

Christiania was divided into a city and a country part. Seámus gave me a lend of his bike and a map to check it all out. I thanked him no end. This was going to be great. Off I toddled with my heart a lot lighter than it'd been entering the place, only half an hour earlier.

Around the corner I couldn't believe my eyes – *loaves* of hashish and great big *sacks* of marijuana – sitting as plain as day on some tables in the sun. I went up to the nearest sack and asked the owner about buying only a little bit of grass. Not a problem. A little bit was fished from the sack and sold for just a few Danish Krone.

While I was there I saw two armed-policemen strolling through the place. This was a major culture shock – the vast amounts of illegal substances openly on display, with the representatives of the law just strolling through. Nice policy, I couldn't help thinking, Dutch coffee shops were one thing, but this was something else.

Anyway, delighted and sorted, I ventured off on Seámus's bike to explore. The first thing that struck me about Christiania was how peaceful it was – no cars, beautiful gardens, colourful murals and loads of laughing kids playing everywhere. For a place with such a dodgy reputation, it sure was tranquil. I followed the map out into the country part, where there was some hairy folk camping by the lake, smiling.

All the buildings had the look of handmade sewn together constructions. But some old façades remained showing the history underneath. I cycled so far that I ended up outside Christiania again. I went up to where the famous Copenhagen mermaid statue is perched on a rock.

It was very small and enclosed by Japanese and American tourists. Fuck that, I thought. Armed with the maps, I made my way up to a hill with a view of the city and sat on a bench.

The sun shone on the water below. It was a lovely moment. I had a joint and sat and read about Christiania. No wonder the Danish Government didn't want to advertise this place – everyone would want to visit. I wrote the inaugural entry in my travel notebook proper…

...where to start...
today is day one travelling on my own
and it's just indescribably amazing.
Buzzing off being tired and
not knowing what to do next...
So much to see... and it's just me...
I'd never been to Copenhagen
before and now I have - but alone -
First time I can say that about anywhere...

After a long while of pontification I trundled back down to the center of Copenhagen, checking out the famous Tivoli Park. I knew the Tivoli Theatre in Dublin, but hadn't ever thought it might have been named after something else somewhere else. Maybe it was named after this place. I don't know.

At about 6ish I brought Seámus back his bike. He wanted to bring me on a pub-crawl around Christiania and Copenhagen, but I had to catch the train to Berlin. I thanked him profusely and headed off.

On the way out of Christiania I saw something freaky. It was just outside the gate near the big sculpture. A man was running down the road with a syringe hanging out of his forehead! It was just dangling down from the skin – really grotesque. He ran wide-eyed past some people, and a woman screamed. Then he was gone. I felt an instant adrenalin rush. Time to go.

4. Berlin

On the train from Copenhagen to Berlin I sat with three other people in the compartment. Two were a young couple from Iceland, and the other was a guy in his thirties from Hungary. We all hit it off really well. None of us had ever met anyone from each other's countries before.

I learnt a few new things; he told us that Budapest used to be two cities, Buda and Pest on either side of the River Danube, and the Icelanders told us that beer was illegal in Iceland up until 1989. That would cause total anarchy in Ireland, I said. We all talked all night.

When we reached Berlin we each went our separate ways. We'd arrived at a station that was in the former East somewhere and I ended up walking for ages. Parts of it still looked like the Soviet Union – grim, bleak, and oppressive. All the same I was fascinated to see the Communist remnants.

Eventually I made it to the west part of the city and started tramming it all over the place. Berlin was fucking big. After hours of knocking around, I stumbled across Potsdamer Platz. At the time it was one big building site, as was much of Berlin. It'd been a central part of the city that'd fallen into no-mans-land and was now being redone. They had an exhibition inside a cylindrical tent of how it would look in the future. I was impressed – history in the making.

After leaving there I walked along a big barren area, which most probably had been where the wall had stood. And behold, all of a sudden I was at the Brandenburg Gate.

It felt momentous. Memories of 1989 flooded back. The world had watched on TV – peace and unification in Germany. It'd been astounding. And here I was at that famous landmark with the wall gone and loads of buildings sprouting up.

On I marched through the Brandenburg Gate and down what's called Unter den Linden. You could just taste the past. Berlin was the zit through which history had been squeezed.

I visited an exhibition of old expensive Daimler automobiles. Capitalism had won for sure. It was clear that Berlin was a city in the midst of massive change, with huge cranes everywhere. East was meeting West bang on.

At one stage I ended up strolling past an Irish Pub called the Oscar Wilde. That had to checked out. Not a bad auld pint. They gave good head. I noted in the notebook that…

… sitting here I've James Joyce, Seán O'Casey, Oscar Wilde, Jonathan Swift, Brendan Behan, George Bernard Shaw, William Butler Yeats, Samuel Beckett, Flann O'Brien, John Synge, Patrick Kavanagh and Oliver Goldsmith all sitting just there over my left shoulder - can't go wrong. It must be a good sign…

Later on, I passed some iffy looking punks who were trying very hard to give it loads of attitude. That was kind of odd. I stifled a laugh because they looked so dated. One of them saw this. For a second I thought they were going to start something. I kept walking. I crossed the street and looked back. One of them shouted something but I couldn't hear with my headphones on. I kept going. Suddenly I felt very alone.

I checked out the Reichstag and then wandered back to the park near the Brandenberg Gate. At this stage I was all historied out. My feet were sore from walking. I had a doze in the sun but didn't quite fall asleep – almost keeping one eye open. It felt nice actually. I'd heard plenty of stories about people coming to no good while travelling, but I reckoned if you kept your wits about you - you'd be all right.

5. Warsaw

The huge building that Stalin built in Warsaw (Warsawa) looked impressive to me, but the locals hated it because Stalin had built it. Fair enough, really. Polish young people seemed effortlessly cool. Like they knew Communism and Capitalism were both bullshit and they didn't give a fuck.

I had visited Warsaw the previous summer. An old Professor from the University had taken a group of us on a city tour. He'd fought in the uprising against the Nazis during the war. He showed us where the battles had happened, where the Jewish Ghetto had been, and where the memorials are now.

He also showed us where they could see the Russian soldiers across the river, watching but not helping. It was humbling. He was so kind and gentlemanly. He really wanted you to know that they fought for a life of freedom that other people maybe take for granted. We took his point. At the same time he drove his Lada like a lunatic.

This year I used public transport. It hadn't changed much since Communist times, like a lot of things. Most of the roads and bridges were badly made and falling to bits. You were in the former Soviet Block and you could tell. You could also see that multi-national corporations were falling over themselves to get their share of the "Zlotys". The advertising here in Poland was more obvious than in the west. It made me realise how saturated Ireland was with advertising, and how we'd become immune to it. Meanwhile in the notebook…

…The lyrics of the songs I'm hearing have become like messages from the netherworld. I'll be thinking about something and then a song lyric will echoe the idea - lovely buzz…

Warsaw was actually the most eastern point of my planned journey. I thought… if somehow I accidentally died now – how long would it take for the body to be shipped home?

6. Krakow

On my train ride from Warsaw to Krakow (Kraków) the farms and fields looked like they hadn't changed in centuries. The people were still using horses for ploughing – echoes of a bygone age and all that. Krakow was stunning. I bought postcards in the square, Rynek Głóny, and took it all in.

Somebody had told me that Hitler had almost wiped out the "intelligentsia" in Poland. What a scary thought that was. These people had amazing resilience. They had endured, despite everything.

Out of pure tourist-ness I checked out the big Catholic Church, which is supposed to be the "be-all-and-end-all". It was amazing Architecture, but a bit daunting. I wondered would Jesus Christ have liked all the merchandise for sale? Or would he have freaked out and thrashed the place, like it says in the bible?

Strolling around, I had a long think about spirituality and prayer and worship and dependency and sheep and opium and the masses and the like. I was talking to myself and loving every minute of it. I stopped and took out the notebook…

…Looking back on what I wrote in Copenhagen, any uneasiness I felt walking around on my own is completely gone now. Thank fuck for that! I was lost but now am found, was down but now am a rolling stone gathering no moss…

I had many more miscellaneous thoughts, ideas and impressions where that came from. For instance… isn't it tempting, when you go somewhere new for the first time, to relate it to somewhere else – to try to make it seem familiar? I thought, isn't the genuine truth that everywhere is unique, but running on the same fuel – love?

7. Auschwitz

A dilapidated bus delivered tourists, including me, from Krakow to Auschwitz (Oświęcim). It took a while and it was really hot and uncomfortable. You couldn't help thinking about what it'd been like for the people who'd been herded here by cattle trains. When the bus stopped we stepped off with a creepy sense of anticipation. Some other tourists were coming out, all quiet and pensive. You could tell they'd been affected by their tour. There was a moody silence in the place.

Our tour group consisted mostly of Americans and Japanese. We walked through the gates that say "Arbeit Macht Frei" (Work makes you free). This set off a load of conflicting thoughts in my head. The sheer nerve of the Nazis to write that – but for the prisoners, working was the only way to survive and maintain any hope of freedom. It was weird being there. I didn't know what to feel.

The weather was lovely and sunny, but it still felt like we were walking on people's graves. We trailed through the dormitories where the people had been crammed together like animals. We passed the wall where people had been shot. Then we entered the building where all the medical experiments had taken place. This place was beyond comprehension.

The walls were covered with photographs of people who had been experimented on. The distortion in the faces and in the eyes of the people was eerie. These people had been treated like guinea pigs. People had been sewn together, limbs swapped - unspeakably horrendous things; fates worse than death. Being there, you felt like a spoilt brat for letting your daily pathetic problems get to you.

Before we got to the Gas Chambers I took a picture of some Japanese Tourists filing through the entrance. I could just picture all those poor people - Jews, Gypsies, Dissidents… a conveyor belt of death. As the group went in I again questioned the logic of us being there. Was this just another tourist destination, or an excursion you'd never forget? Was it an experience that could change your life?

Inside the Gas Chamber itself was particularly ominous. You couldn't help feeling humility just for being free and living a free life. And having just seen the human experimentation, you could imagine how death might even have been a relief.

We were also shown the place where a lot of people had been hanged. After the war the Nazi commandant who had been in charge of Auschwitz was executed here. That gave everybody in the tour group a strange feeling of satisfaction – as if one death made up for all the others. There was some awkward shuffling. I found the whole thing to be completely unreal – people just paced around in disbelief. You really didn't know what to feel. You were numbed by the place.

We left Auschwitz as contemplative as the other tourists we'd seen leaving earlier. The bus ferried us back to civilization and everyone dispersed. Nobody could be left unaffected by that experience. Some people had gone on to Birkenau (the other city of death nearby) but that was enough doom and gloom for one day. I felt honoured to be free, and to be on this trip. I had to write something…

…Auschwitz was an indescribable eye-opener,
the scale of it, all those innocent faces,
the cramped conditions, the shooting wall.
It's all too much to take in – sensory overload –
but definitely worth visiting. Fucking hell…

I thought – surely Hitler was evil? And hadn't Stalin killed even more people, and Chairman Mao even more again? And what about the Belgians, British, Dutch, French, Portuguese and Spanish in Africa, America and Asia? Not to mention the I.R.A. killing innocent people indiscriminately. Didn't every nation have blood on its hands? Auschwitz was another example of the atrocities in everyone's past. History belonged to all of us. We were all to be blamed and praised alike…

It was time to move on. The internal monologue in my head was too much. The whole thing had been beyond belief. Fuck…

8. Prague

ARE
SAYING
FRIDA

Prague (Praha) is the capital of Bohemia, home of the bohemian lifestyle. I got there early in the morning, and headed straight for a hostel where one of the lads was supposed to be staying. And indeed someone from Ireland with his surname was staying there but not he. So I wandered back off. This had brought me up to the top of one of the hills (Prague is built on nine hills, two more than Rome). This hill had a football stadium on it, and Status Quo were playing soon ("The status quo wouldn't've allowed that a few years earlier." I groaned). The bus journey up and down the hill had blown my mind. Prague was pretty pretty.

Czech people had loads of style. There were Eva Herzagova look-alikes everywhere – bless them. I strolled on over the Charles Bridge and around the old town listening to The Orb's "Voyages Beyond the Underworld" and conversing with myself. It felt brilliant.

So I walked and walked and lapped it all up. I'd read how Prague was one of the only major capital cities in Europe not to have been heavily bombed in the war, and how the Architecture had three different styles from three different eras that no other city had, apparently.

I ambled around in awe gaping at the buildings, then got on a tram and travelled as far as it went, and back. The outskirts were a strange mix of beautiful old buildings and horrible modern constructions. When I got back to the centre I had a wander up and down the big boulevard, which, spectacularly, was called "Václavské náměsti". Crazy.

There were loads of people selling loads of stuff, including one guy selling bongs, pipes and rolling papers. On the spur of the moment I asked him if he had anything to put in the pipe. He said yeah and showed me some meshes.

So I looked him in the eye. "Ah!" said he, glanced both ways, and sold me a little lump of Afghani hashish. That'll do nicely, said I.

All day I'd been traipsing around, so I went for a meal in a touristy (but nice) café. It was cool; I ended up getting chatting to a nice American couple. Worryingly, they were convinced that the gap between the "haves" and "have-nots" is so big in America that it could get violent and nasty – like the L.A. riots only worse. I hoped they were wrong.

After the meal I rolled a nice big joint in the toilet, bid the cool Americans farewell and headed to the riverbank with a spring in my step. It must be difficult being American, I thought. The hash kicked in. I found myself on an emotional roller coaster once again. Thankfully I had the notebook with me.

By the banks of the Vistula I sat down and started writing. I felt inspired. And Why Not? I wrote down "Why Not?" This was going to be the name of my book "Why Not?" I had so much that I wanted to record on paper – impressions, incidents, views, characters, dogs, babes, bikes, buildings, fountains, posters, cafés, streets, strangers, trams, tramps. There was way too much to write. You'd have to be sparing in your choice of words. But sure wasn't I in a Bohemian mood? I wrote in the notebook there and then…

IT'S ALL IN THE MIND

It's all in the mind

Eee…oh…me…ad…eo

It's all in the mind!

More and more, when I went to write in my notebook, whatever I wrote would end up either rhyming or being visual in some way. And so I decided this would be what would come out of my holiday: a book of visual poetry inspired by all the impressions of the trip. I was delighted and excited – and why not?

There was nothing for it but to go for a celebratory Czech beer. The proceeding mini-pub-crawl saw three different beer prices – 39, 22 and 15 koruna – cheaper as you got further from the center of the city.

In one district I stumbled across streets with loads of small art galleries that were open at night. It seemed a real hotbed of creative activity. There were Frank Zappa posters everywhere. He had been appointed Cultural Ambassador by the Czech Government and was therefore a bit of a cult hero here.

Somewhere along the way the next day I came across the John Lennon wall, up on one of the hills. The wall consisted of a shrine-like graffiti montage of Lennonisms, portraits and messages. It seemed to really mean something here in a place where people had had so little hope.

I'd wanted to fill in my journal about everything that'd happened but too much was happening. I just had to let it all happen – and live it all up; and live up to living it up.

Yet another tram took me to a terminal out in the arse end of nowhere. I tried speaking some pigeon Polish, and it was similar enough to Czech for the nice lady working there to understand. She appreciated the effort. It made my day.

In the afternoon I got a bus right out to the outskirts again – where the real people live. I went into a real person's bar. There was motorcycle racing on the TV.

Eight locals sat at the bar with beer, and a cute Bohemian barmaid with lots of cleavage smiled from behind the counter. Lovely. After a meal and a beer and a fleeting flirt with the barmaid, I was off. You wouldn't want to push it.

9. Budapest

The train passed through Bratislava, the capital of Slovakia. Things were getting seriously foreign. We got to Budapest at about six in the morning. I was all excited getting off the train. Hungary! This was going to be something else.

As I stepped onto the platform an Irish accent asked if I needed hostel accommodation. He was from Waterford. Whoa, I wasn't expecting that. For fuck's sake, y' can't go anywhere…

Anyway I made my way into Budapest proper and walked the place silly. The River Danube was amazing. Here it was called the Duna. Magyar, which is Hungarian for 'Hungarian', is unique among European languages, except that it has similarities to Finnish, for some reason.

Anyway after hiking around I stopped in a little café/bar type thing. Annie Lennox was singing on the radio; something about travelling the world looking for something. I was looking for a beer. Fuck it, I was on holiday. I sat there and wrote in my notebook and drank three beers between the hours of 10 and 12 in the a.m. Sure if you can't do things like that when you're on holiday, when can y'?

I was tipsy on the Hungarian beer, so I buzzed around thinking, fucking hell I'm in Hungary – little old me – the Austro-Hungarian Empire and all that – the Danube – the massive buildings along the river. Flipping heck.

Somehow I found a hostel and spent the afternoon catching up on sleep. The train-sleeping thing wasn't so restful. I thought about the Hungarian guy on the train from Copenhagen to Berlin, and the couple from Iceland. We'd all learnt something new that night. And now here I was now in his country. Nice one. You'd never imagine yourself in Hungary. At the hostel I collapsed into bed and slept the sleep of a thousand drowsy babies.

Waking up I remembered that I was in Budapest. Wow! A guy called Stephan from Munich was my hostel roommate for the evening. He was inter-railing too. We had a pleasant conversation. He was pretty conservative, and I thought that both of us were seeing different things in the same places. Still, we had a good laugh.

After a while he headed off sight seeing. I stayed and relaxed in the twilight and caught up with the notebook...

...It's mad how the time is going –
it flies in a way, but when eye'm tired
or whatever – like last night after having
toured Prague for ten hours – it dragged.
Sure it's all relative – as Einstein'd say...

At about 8ish I ventured down to the riverfront with the cool edifices. They were all lit up at night. One of the old castles looked as if it had been literally carved out of the cliff face. The weather was weird. It wasn't too hot, about 25° Celsius, but it was stifling. There was a thunderstorm brewing, and the whole valley was full of atmospheric activity. I walked up the Castle Hill to get a better view of the whole scenario.

At the top the view was unreal. It was a serious collection of buildings along the river. Then the thunderstorm started kicking in. You could sense that the rain would begin soon. So I headed for a tram station. Just as I got underneath the tram shelter the heavens opened. I made it back into the central area and had a gander around what's called "Vörösmarty tér" – another nicely peculiar language.

Thankfully the rain stopped quickly. But I was starting to get tired now, and was feeling slightly vulnerable. It occurred to me that I'd be pretty defenseless if attacked at this moment. I'm in fucking Hungary, for fuck's sake. I'd been lucky so far. So it was time for bed.

The next day I explored further afield. You'd know that Budapest had been the centre of an Empire. What kind of strange goings-on had gone on here?

I kept seeing beggars on the streets that were disfigured in some way. Was this something to do with the former Communist regime, or was it the vicinity to like, Chernobyl? Or was I just imagining it?

In the evening I went to the island in the middle of the river. I found a nice solitary spot, set down my bag, took out my juggling balls and had a juggle. I'd made a point of juggling everyday. It's good for you, they say, one of the few activities where you use both sides of the brain.

Lying down in the sunshine, it felt like I was on summer holiday, not your typical package deal but something tailor made. I thought about all the people I loved and missed. This was the seventh city and the fifth country I'd been in since leaving Amsterdam seven days ago. Whoa. Oh look, some hairy-arm-pitted ladies. It's true, travel does broaden the mind.

10. Vienna

EDLE EINFALT
STILLE UND GRÖßE!!

My plan was to sleep on the train overnight on the way to Vienna (Wien) – just like I'd done from Copenhagen to Berlin, Krakow to Prague, and Prague to Budapest. Unfortunately Vienna was nearer to Budapest than I'd thought. The train arrived in Vienna at three in the morning – a slight oversight. The train station was closing, so I had to have a wander around suburban Vienna in the middle of the night.

So be it. I came across a building site. Behind a fence on some grass I lay down to fall asleep – sleeping rough, the easy way. I lay there feeling like a hypocrite. The weather was really mild. Would this be the only time you'd ever sleep on the street? Well, lucky fucking you. How easy you have it.

Anyway I lay there thinking about this, and did kind of sleep a bit for about an hour or so. I was so tired I could've literally slept anywhere. When the train had arrived early I'd been in a deep sleep. I was like a half sleeping zombie looking for anywhere to fall back into slumber.

It was a clear night and the stars were out. After a while I got up and walked around a bit. I tried to catch some more sleep on a bench but failed. So I wrote in the notebook…

…It's mad - every day so far on this trip
I've felt a feeling of sheer elation,
and I've only myself to share it with…

At about 6ish I made my way back to the station and got the train to central Vienna. Everybody I'd had contact with so far was lovely and smiley. Austria was nice. I got some Schillings and drank a coffee, savouring every last drop. Armed with the guide book I soldiered on.

"Der Ring" thing that they have in Vienna was the longest line of consistently impressive architecture I'd ever seen. It was absurd, almost bordering on obscene. It was also majestic. That was the word that kept springing to mind: majestic.

On the train I'd been reading *Schindler's Ark*. A lot of the story had actually happened in some of the places I'd visited – Berlin, Krakow, Auschwitz. Oskar Schindler had originally come from the Sudetenland in (former) Czechoslovakia.

And the bad guy had actually come from Austria. I thought about the dormitories in Auschwitz in comparison to all this lavish Viennese architecture. It didn't bear thinking about.

While exploring down by the river I discovered some amazing graffiti. One of them looked like it was three-dimensional. I actually had to go up and touch it to make sure that it was two-dimensional. It had just been really well shaded by the artist. It was seriously striking. I'd read that Vienna had the highest percentage of over-forty-year-olds of any European capital. This, I reckoned, had been the spray painting of an under-forty-year-old. But then again, you never know.

11. Innsbruck

The journey by train through the Alps to Innsbruck was just stunning. I hadn't had much experience of real mountains before so the Alps were a major novelty. Every few seconds there was another incredible view. It was like an advertisement. In Ireland we had some large hills that we called mountains, but this was the real thing.

There were two Austrian guys on the train. We got chatting. Skiing was their buzz. They didn't care too much for football, but they laughed a lot and were good fun. We passed through Salzburg, home of Mozart. I would've liked to stop there if time had permitted. But it left something to do next time.

The train got to Innsbruck at about four in the evening. Outside the train station there was an Alp behind every building. Wacky! The other impression I got was that folk weren't short of a few Schillings here. There were no beggars on these streets.

The river Inn in Innsbruck was actually a lovely silvery green colour, with the water coming straight on down from the Alps. I hadn't seen that colour river before; it seemed otherworldly. One of the lads from Ireland was supposed to end up travelling through this place at some stage. Had he been here already? Was he here now? Or was he coming in the future? It felt kind of strange. Was I going to turn a corner and bump into him? The notebook remained my sole companion…

… Innsbruck - this place is seriously quaint, lots of expensive cars, lots of expensive shops, lots of expensive people. It's the exact opposite of the East - poor people must be just a rumour. What have the Alps seen that we can't imagine?

On "Universitätsstrasse" I remembered that Innsbruck held a winter Olympics once, which by default makes it sophisticated. It was kind of spooky. You felt like apologizing for not being rich enough. By the time the train left Innsbruck it felt like I'd been in Austria for a week – not a day.

12. Florence

In the train compartment was a history teacher, Chris from Bradford, who was also touring Europe. We compared notes and agreed it was all mad, then fell asleep. I woke up in Florence (Firenze) realising that I had to get off the train immediately. So I grabbed all my stuff – runners, bag, notebook, and food – and jumped off the train. I waved goodbye to Chris. He was off to Rome, to do as the Romans.

Looking around I realised that this couldn't be the centre. Another suburb? OK then, first things first: where's the toilet? I put on my runners and flung all the stuff in the bag. The toilet was just a little hole on the floor where you're supposed to squat and do your thing. I decided I could wait.

So I got the next train in what I thought would be the direction of central Florence, but actually led to a place called Montevarchi. It was a beautiful spot. The platform was filling up with real live Italian people going to work. Gradually Italians speaking Italian surrounded me. It felt *magnifico.*

The train back towards Florence was full of conversations. I tried to understand, and couldn't. Still, *Forza Italia!* We passed a huge field of sleeping sunflowers– it felt like being in an Italian postcard. I still managed to get off at a station that wasn't the main one, and had to walk for ages to get to the centre. Oh well. I saw loads of urban Italian life – lots of Fiats and Alfa Romeos and coffee machines.

Walking along I had a flash realisation that yesterday I was in Austria, the day before I was in Hungary, today I was in Italy, and tomorrow I'd be in Germany. Wow – this really was a dream come true.

I walked for miles (kilometres, even) and was beginning to feel a bit feeble, so I had a cappuccino. Bella. Eventually I found the centre of the city. It was unbelievable – loads of stuff you'd recognise from TV: the ridiculously big church, the bridge, the whole nine yards.

Somehow I bumped into two auld ones from Ireland (Galway and Donegal) and one of their daughters. They were lost, and flustered. I helped them with their map. They weren't handling the heat too well and were a bit culture shocked.

I was culture shocked out of it like a good thing by this stage. Waking up everyday in a new country with different currencies and languages was all new to me.

At one stage I walked into an Italian fruit shop and said, "Bonjourno". *Buon Giorno*, they said. "Duo banana?" *Prego.* "Grazie, Arrivederci!…" The whole thing was in Italian. The lady laughed. I was delighted. *Bellissimo!*

For lunch I ate three different bread-ham-cheese combinations from an Italian bakery. *Perfecto!* Walking through the Piazza eating Pizza, I felt a million Lire. I stopped for a coffee, accidentally ordering a tiny little thing. The old couple who owned the café were lovely, like something out of a Felini film (not that I'd seen a Felini film, but what you'd reckon people in Felini films looked like).

Anyway, there was no shortage of beautiful women in Florence, unless you were a smelly Irish itinerant. I was so tired that only the notebook could help now…

…Well, well, well, am eye fucking knackered? An experimental state of mind - a - go - go! Sleep depravation'll do strange things to a man. I'm laughing my arse off at myself. Today's the day, that if I was travelling with someone else, I'd be a headfuck to be with. Lucky I'm alone…

While I was walking around the cobblestone streets, a total babe on a scooter came scooting around the corner. It was all seriously Italian. Big time. It felt like it was a privilege to be there. Italy was an amazing country. It'd be great to stay for a couple of weeks or more. Anyway, now it was on to Venice!

At the station I saw the maddest thing – a guy who worked for the railway was sorting luggage on the platform, and a pretty lady and her boyfriend were getting off a train. The railway guy started wolf whistling and gesturing like fuck (literally) at the woman. He was really out of order. In Ireland this situation would already have been a fight. But the boyfriend just walked on by with his lady. The railway guy, work on hold temporarily, kept right on howling like a wolf. I was shocked.

13. Venice

It was a really pleasant journey from Florence up to Venice (Venizzia). I was in love with being in Italy. The train arrived in the newer part of Venice, which meant getting another train out to the actual old and famous bit. It was right out in the Adriatic Sea. When I got there it was like a Hollywood set, except it was authentic.

There were loads of tourists, mostly American and Japanese as usual. I wandered around and took everything in. It was beyond description. I went back and had a shower at the train station, washing away the dirt of Hungary, Austria and Italy. I couldn't maintain this train-sleeping thing at the current pace.

Anyway I explored Venice, feeling truly "lonesome" for the first time on my trip. I couldn't help feeling that this place should really be experienced with a lover. ("Showering more often might help", I laughed to myself).

I ended up off the beaten track of tourist paraphernalia. It was the old residential part, where real people lived and travelled around by boat and stuff.

There was some classical music floating from somebody's window, so I sat on some steps beside a canal and listened. Somewhere else a couple started arguing, or maybe just talking, you couldn't tell. I was enjoying the whole situation, this Venetian scenario, so much. So I notebooked away…

…A serious day of extremes… this morning feeling like absolute shite and now I'm feeling all that elation I was talking about yesterday – by fuck I'm happy! I can't wait to see the state of my head when I get to Bamberg tomorrow…

In the Marco Polo Restaurant beside a canal in Venice I had a meal – postcardsville once more. I had just enough Italiano money for a no-frills pizza without a drink. Signor Waiter wasn't overly impressed with me not wanting a drink. But by buying the pizza, I'd made him an offer he couldn't refuse. *Si?*

14. Bamberg

No fewer than three of the lads from Ireland were working and living in Bamberg, Germany at this time. We had a mad time of it, so we did. I had an amazing chat with a cute German girl (who had a boyfriend – one of the lads) about life, the universe and everything – and indeed *The Hitchhiker's Guide to the Galaxy*. She talked about broadening your mind, and looking at the big picture.

That night we went to a little beer festival in the mountains, where an old man made beer with schnapps in it. It was ludicrously strong. One beer and you're drunk. We had several, and ended up playing guitar and keyboards. Luckily we couldn't remember much the next day.

The guitar of the people who'd been playing had been totally out of tune but nobody had noticed. Everybody was hammered, except for the designated drivers who must've found it very bizarre. It was bizarre either way. People were really letting their hair down. Once a year the old man sells his extra strong beer, and that's the festival. It's well known for being a fervent event – and, amazingly, no hangover!

There was lots and lots of talking with the lads that weekend. Ideas were thrown around. "Does everything happen for a reason?" and the like. The theme I'd adopted in the notebook was that of "Fucking Off" in lots of different ways. Fucking off, way off, till you found the perspective you needed. Fucking off in the sense of doing something that was fuck-offy – against the grain, outside the box. Not only pushing the envelope but fucking off with it.

We talked philosophy and art and bullshit and football and music and… we touched on most subjects probably. I fell asleep talking. I hadn't talked to anybody about what I'd seen on my travels so far, and there was no shutting me up. I woke up talking.

All this was taking its toll on the lads, but they were taking it well. Clearly I was a tad over-enthusiastic. Still, we all laughed a lot that weekend. But on Sunday it was time to go on, and so on I went. The lads saw me off at the train station. I was going to be back in a week's time for the Bamberg Bier Fest. Nice.

Re-reading through the journal on the train I nearly cried with delight at having got this far and experienced all these things. It was all getting fierce emotional. I wrote in the notebook…

Spontaneous Poem No. 4,444

With so much to say
There's just no way
To tell it all – it's tough,
Yet the fact that I want to
Share the lot
Is, in itself, enough*.

(*Not all, just most, so enough.)

(This phrase "Not all, just most, so enough." kept cropping up in what I was writing. Fuck knows why.) On the way back up to Amsterdam I was on a brand new super cool German train. I was very impressed, especially having camped on Eastern European trains for the best part of a week.

15. Amsterdam Again

Apparently Amsterdam is one of the few cities in Europe where more than 50% of the people living there are non-native. I was thrilled to be back. This was a kind of homecoming; the first leg of the journey had been completed. I had to pick up a paycheck and then I was off again. Walking through Central Station I was buzzing off all the diversity. There were travelling stories everywhere. I was just another grain of sand.

After getting a rent-a-bike I headed over the canal, straight up Damrak and checked the Geldautomat. I'd been paid. Lovely. I swung a left at the Grasshopper, another right past the sex shops, and left again to the Feels Good coffee shop.

I sat outside on the steps in front of the canal and had a joint, reviewing in my mind the big circle that I'd just made: Amsterdam, Copenhagen (and Christiania), Warsaw, Krakow, Auschwitz, Prague, Budapest, Vienna, Innsbruck, Florence, Venice, Bamberg, and Amsterdam again. So that meant that this was my seventh country and twelfth city in fourteen days. And I still had two weeks to go.

Once again I got the feeling of being honoured, that this was a privilege, compared to people like Anne Frank, and all the others who didn't have the chance to live their lives to the full. In Bamberg we'd talked about how lucky our generation was to be living during the longest period of peace in Europe ever, by a long shot. Any violence in our lives was urban.

Luckily, there'd been no nasty situations so far on the trip. There was that strange moment with those punks in Berlin. And I'd felt the potential for trouble that night in Budapest, but had legged it back to the hostel. Maybe my Granny was looking after me from the afterlife (if there was an afterlife, after all).

Anyway, I was sitting there outside the Feels Good and it was all running through my head. I just felt so fulfilled and energised and vibed-up and that sort of thing. I didn't know what to do, laugh or cry, or both.

Out came the trusty notebook. I flicked through it… Whoa. I'd never be able to explain to anybody how all this felt. How many cities in how many days? How many countries? OK, this is what I had wished for, and worked for. I was gonna have to surf this wave all the way to the beach (man!).

So there I was with all this going on in my brain. Suddenly I got an overwhelming urge to write a poem. Across the way a woman was sitting in the sun with her eyes closed. She was being extremely calm and chilled out in a pretty seedy neighbourhood of Amsterdam. Her serenity amid the chaos was amazing to watch. I decided to write her a spontaneous poem. Prior to this trip, I wasn't in the habit of writing poetry at people, but it was the kind of thing that was happening more and more…

Poem for a Stranger

I'm compelled to words
On this the 4th last
Day of Summer 1995
So alive - and kicking
It's almost sickening.
Love, from a Stranger.

With that, I grabbed my stuff and cycled over to her, gave her the poem, smiled, then was off before she could even read it. She smiled a surprised smile. I just felt so alive that I had to share it with someone, and she had stuck out like a sore thumb by being so discreet and serene.

I cycled along the sunny side of the canal and swung a right up towards Dam Square. When I got to the middle of the square I stood there with the bike, a million thoughts running through my mind. Something was changing. I experienced an overwhelming… overwhelming-ness! It felt like I was IN the moment. I'd never felt like this before. All I could do was observe – intrigued, excited and confused.

I cycled down towards the cheap supermarket. Along the way the people were starting to look like caricatures of themselves. I didn't know what to think, so I just kept on going.

At the supermarket I got some food and stocked up with beer for all the gang in the campsite. But my bearings were elsewhere. Looking at a tree through the only window in the supermarket, I thought - what the fuck is going on in my head?

I got to the checkout. There were lots of people, mostly fellow immigrants buying cheap groceries. As I was putting my stuff in a bag, a young boy accidentally dropped a jar of jam on the floor. A strange old man shouted at the boy in Dutch. He was out of order. The kid looked at me and looked at the spilt jam, and said in English – "What should I do?" I said – "Someone is paid to clean it up, so you just go home if you want." The kid smiled and legged it off. The old man was unimpressed. Two big black ladies in the queue nudged each other and grinned. I went on out and loaded the bike basket with beer.

Suddenly everything came to a head, my head. Before I knew what was going on, I was standing there with the bike lock and key in my hands… having just uttered something in an awed whisper. Seriously! The words that came out of my mouth were "Putting things into words". I heard what I'd said after I said it. To be honest, it freaked the fucking shit out of me. I just stood there speechless, not knowing what was happening. Was I going mad?

That's when the two black ladies walked past, and one of them let out a laugh that only big black ladies can do – a big joyous cackle. I laughed back. Man, whatever the fuck it was that was going on, it was definitely good. That was for sure. I'd had mind-expanding experiences before, but this was something beyond all that. This was some previously untapped part of my mind, or some such thing. What the…?

"Putting things into words"? The phrase hit me like a brick. And it made sense in plenty of ways. Putting into words where it is that we're going wrong, or something like that. It made sense but I couldn't explain to myself why. The words kept ringing through me. On I went.

I cycled on up past the Fatal Flower Coffee Shop and underneath the Rijksmuseum. Hmm, "Putting things into words"; I could do that. What in the name of fuck was this all about? If it wasn't supposed to happen it wouldn't have happened. Okay, I had to just cycle to the campsite. I swung through Vondel Park to soak up some Amsterdam atmosphere. For some reason I decided to take a short cut across the grass beside the lake. But the ground got unexpectedly bumpy. Beer cans started falling from the basket. Shit. I'd been going pretty fast.

Various vagrants descended on the beer cans like vultures. I had no choice but to say "Cheers!" and be off. Adrenalin rush once again. I got out of the park and onto the road for the Amsterdamse Bos.

The forest, my old friend, welcomed me with open branches. The best things in life are free. Little amuses the simple. I was floating on air. All these events were flashing through my brain. "Putting things into words…" and I'd whispered it and THEN heard it… What on earth...?

Nothing had ever felt like this before. By this stage I was riding in familiar forest territory, so I leaned back and cycled with no hands and thought, "what the fff…?" Then these words came from my mouth – "Oh Lord". It was another subconscious outburst. But this time I thought, heard, and said the words simultaneously. I really thought, oh no, am I losing it here?

"Lord"? This one did not go down well at all. It made no sense, whatsoever. The whole "worship" thing was very messed up. All that God-fearing was daft. I definitely wasn't sold on the whole God thing, but I didn't really know what to think. All the people wanting you to believe in them seemed like they needed it too much.

I could sense that what I was sensing was unorthodox, to say the least. This was, as far as I was concerned, the unknown in a way that I'd never known it. It'd always been obvious what was true and what wasn't, but this whatnot would not be forgot…

What was I thinking? I was buzzed up and convinced that I was the most unique person on earth, which of course everyone is. And that was the thing, it felt amazingly good to be alive, and I could sense that everybody could feel this good, that we are all equal in this amazingness. Everyone is as amazing as the next man (and woman, and child). And so on and so forth… It was all so damned lovely - I wouldn't have wanted to be someone else for anything. This was it, living life to the full, seeing new things, experiencing new experiences. But what the hell was that with the "Putting things into words" thing? And now the "Lord" thing? It scared me but it fascinated me. It excited but worried me. Scary but fascinating, exciting but worrying, odd yet natural. Was I coming to no good, or know good? Oh man…

Eventually I got to the campsite and cycled into the Irish Field. Everybody was just arriving home from work – party time! I was brought back down to earth. Camping - back to nature. There was lots of camaraderie and shenanigans. Unbelievably there was a band from Dun Laoghaire playing in a club in Amsterdam that night, which was a very nice coincidence.

Later on I tried telling the story of what had happened with the subconscious whispering thing and all, but I couldn't quite believe it myself. All the same, there was something to it. It kept nagging at me. The next day in the shower I thought about it. It can't be a "Religious" thing, that whole trip was a bad buzz. It was something bigger t**han** t**ha**t **ha ha**…

How was I supposed to put these things into words? This is when the notebook entries changed from recording what was going on around me, to recording what was going on in my head. I was surprised to have survived this journey as it was progressing, and it was getting madder and madder.

But I knew it was all meant to happen, as it happens. It all felt good, mostly, even if it was a bit confusing. I mused, and ruminated, and reflected, and deliberated, and pontificated, and contemplated, and considered, and brooded, and chewed it all over. I was really so fortunate to be doing all this, and obliged to enjoy the shit out of it.

Putting things into words? The theme of the trip had been fucking off. I loved the phrase "fuck off". It said it all really. It was a great leveller. Billy Connolly said that you never read, "Fuck Off, *he hinted…*" Slowly but surely the "fucking off" theme developed into fully-fledged "Fuck Off-ism"!

Fuck "ism's" – except optimism, realism and maybe a few others. Fuck all these lies we're being told from birth till death, by various non-truth-telling parties, about what we should and shouldn't do, and how we should and shouldn't do it.

Fuck the accepted norm. Fuck the status quo. Fuck the undemocratic United Nations. Fuck narrow-mindedness. Fuck fuddy-duddies. Fuck, indeed, the system, fuck censorship, fuck taboos, fuck decorum, fuck corruption, fuck, for that matter, corporations. And while we're at it – fuck convention, fuck conditioning, fuck prejudice, fuck aggression, fuck mindlessness, fuck cynicism, and yes, fuck the begrudgers. Fuck this, that and the other. Fuck not questioning everything. Fuck, the toilets must be around here somewhere, man…

16. Gent

KUNST

On to Gent I went. There was a nice friendly mother and child on the train. She was a French speaking Belgian and spoke with a lovely lilt. When she mentioned the European Union she called it "The Community", which was cool. I gave her a poem on the spur of the moment. She smiled.

A gent in Gent, I had a "mastel" doughnut and a Café au Lait. The little differences between the countries were kicking in again... Everything in Holland (outside Amsterdam) seemed straight. Belgium was kind of like a mixture between Holland and France. Sometimes it felt Dutch, sometimes French. But most of the time it was just Belgium. So I bought some Belgian chocolate, as you do. When in Gent, and all that.

The guide book said that in the course of history the Belgians had been ruled by the Romans, French, Spanish, Austrians, Dutch, English, and Germans. And we Irish thought we had it bad. And of course Belgium had been ransacked in the wars. I thought of all the people who had lost their lives needlessly fighting someone else's war – a whole generation wasted, for what? Our generation had known a period of peace that no other had known, and did we appreciate it? Fuck War. I notebooked...

...Do you need to be respected by people
who are messed up in the head?
Do you want to be admired by
a society that's fucked up in general?
How can these things be put into words?
Paraphraseology, feckology, fuckology...

I badly needed to calm down, but it wasn't going to happen. Both sides of the brain argued with each other the whole time. I was inspired, brimming with ideas, overflowing with gusto, dying to somehow articulate this onslaught of thoughts, to put it into words.

17. Antwerp

The Belgians are very good at beer. Arriving in Antwerp I felt like Captain of the Universe. I was on this whole buzz of "I've just travelled through nine countries alone and survived, and therefore am completely IT". And then of course there was the whole "strange unexplained experience in Amsterdam". Not to mention "Fuck Off-ism".

I bounded down the main street of Antwerp taking it all in, breathing in the buildings, smelling the coffee. I was suffering from delusions of grandeur. Stopping at a beautiful café, I made a note – which refused not to rhyme…

Now And Then

Now then, where was eye?
Well eye was a lot of places,
Buildings, cars, mostly faces
And the farther eye went
& the harder eye pushed IT
The more or less success
Getting things off the chest
At the behest of something inside.
You can run but you just can't hide...

Hmmm… I continued on down the boulevard, stopping in a café for a Belgian beer in a nice Belgian beer glass. I started thinking about countries and their beers; Guinness in Ireland, Heineken in Holland, Żywiec in Poland, Budwar in Czech, 523,000,000 beers in Germany, … if religion is the opiate of the masses, what's alcohol? The lubricant? And what's war - a culling of the masses? I don't know.

For dinner I dined in an American type diner, had some Mexican option and beer from a smiling waitress called Zuby. On I wandered back up to the big grandiose train station - another café; another lovely waitress. I wondered back to what had happened in Amsterdam. There was a change going on in my mind, beyond the thoughts I'd had before. It was all uncharted territory, but somehow I got the gist.

18. Brussels

The centre of Brussels (Brouxelles) was cobblestoney and dark. I got there at about 11 at night, walked out of the station and straight into a big hotel. I don't really know why I did this, but for some reason I did, just following my intuition.

In I went and asked how much it was for a room. It was way too many Belgian Francs for little old me. The guy behind the counter was young and seemed cool.

It was a big old foyer with sofas, high ceilings and a grand piano. There was nobody around. I asked him if I could have a go on the piano. He said "Sure, but don't be too loud".

So I played the only two things I knew how to play properly: Gerswhin's Summertime and The Entertainer by Scott Joplin. It felt amazing to be sitting there playing this beautiful instrument, after just getting to Brussels.

I stopped playing before I messed anything up, and then thanked the guy who gave a clap and smiled a toothy grin.

Off I skipped into the night with a distinct bounce in my step. I had a quick look around and then found a cheap hotel. No sleeping on a train tonight.

The room had a view over the old rooftops. I felt like a king in his castle. With all sorts of different languages talking away on the TV, it really seemed like this was the middle of Europe.

I turned off the TV and all the lights in the room and lay on the bed. I was still reeling from the quasi-dimensional spiritual experience that had happened in Amsterdam. Something was telling me not to dwell on it, just enjoy the moment. That had been the point. Go with it. Seize the day, as they say.

So seize I did. The next day I walked Brussels stupid, saw all the main touristy bits (which were impressively beautiful), and found out that the inventor of the saxophone was Belgian. You learn something new every day.

All the while the various happenings were whirling around in my mind. It seemed that one way or another, I had happened upon something that not everyone gets to happen upon. At least that's how it felt to me at the time. The notebook was getting weirder and weirder…

Verse More Won

one more verse

verse vica

vica verse

It's a curse

needs a nurse

could be worse

time heals

all fuck offs

time fuck's off

fuck off time

time to fuck off...

And then there was the whole "brain" thing. I kept having all these thoughts about the left and right sides of the brain, and how we don't use them. It was a known scientific fact that humans only use a small fraction of their mind. If this was so, why did we still all have the same education systems as always? Why didn't we come up with something better? Maybe it was because we were only using a small fraction of our minds.

19. Paris

I was overjoyed and ecstatic when the train pulled into Paris. I'd never been there before, and now that I was doing so much writing it all seemed to be coming together. This was where Joyce, Beckett, Hemmingway, Picasso, Dali, Wilde and many more lunatics did their thing. And here I was now doing my thing. It felt like I was in a film or something.

On the way down on the train I'd been writing in the notebook like a man possessed. A group of young French guys sat opposite me. One of them asked me what I was writing. I'd been thinking and grinning to myself and scribbling away, so I told him I was writing "Fuck Off-ist" poetry.

This made him smile. We got chatting. I asked them where would be a good spot to get some grass in Paris. They said to have a gander around La Bastille at night. I said I would.

After arriving, I walked around for ages and ages and ages. I found a window table in a corner café and relaxed, feeling all full of myself and over-confident. As I sat there, an absolute mega-babe walked into the bar: tall, blonde, skinny-in-a-model-type-way, beautifully dressed – just an exceptionally attractive individual. And I was sitting there thinking to myself - Go up and talk to her. Why not? Y' know. Never before would I have had the confidence to just walk up and talk to someone that beautiful, but I thought – why not now?

So I went up to her and said – Hi, do you speak English? And she said – Yes. So I said - Would you like to join me for a drink? And she said - Well yeah sure but let's stay here at the bar because it costs less than sitting at a table. So I said – Ok, I didn't know that.

We stayed at the bar and we started talking. I told her what I was doing; that I was travelling Europe and that my theme was "Fucking Off". She was interested so I ended up showing her some of the Fuck Off-ist poetry, and she actually liked it – it made her laugh. We kind of clicked a bit.

She had just finished a hard days modeling – she *was* a model, a catwalk model if you don't mind. The whole time we were chatting I couldn't believe that I'd actually talked to her. I was thinking – even though she's exceptionally attractive she's a normal person really.

We talked and talked for a good couple of hours. We were getting on really well and I was thinking – Wow - I've waited to meet a woman and here I am talking to this angel of a goddess! She asked could she keep one of the poems – it was one about "fucking relationships" – and how ships are something to fuck off on. So I tore it out of my notebook and she put it in her wallet.

One thing led to another and (I can't remember exactly how we got around to it in the conversation but) she said – Well, you know, if you don't flirt you'll never get laid. And I thought – Whoa, here we go! And she said she just lived around the corner, so I said - Why don't we go back and we can just hang out and she was like – Yeah, why not?

Anyway, we'd been talking about hash, and she said it'd be nice to smoke a joint. One of the guys at the bar said he could sort out some hash if someone drove him to get it, and she was like – Yeah, no problem.

So we hopped in her car – me, her and the other guy – and drove across the Seine. As we did we saw the Eiffel Tower all lit up beside the river and it looked magical. Then I, like a complete ejit, fucked things up. She said something like – You never know what could happen. And I said something like – My friend told me about you – meaning – You're the woman I've been waiting to meet (because one of the lads had said I'd meet someone soon), which of course probably creeped her out completely. Not that I realised, I was wired to the moon.

But she said nothing and drove on. So we scored some hash and had a smoke. She felt tired and suggested finding me a hotel. She did all the talking in French at the hotel, and we arranged to meet in the same bar the next day.

I went up to my room and felt like I was God's gift to the world, thinking – I've got the secret of the universe and found the woman of my dreams. I stayed up late smoking and writing. All the next day I was thinking – Wow, I'm actually going to meet up with her later – I'm such a lucky guy…

Funnily enough, when I went to meet her at the bar – she didn't turn up. I stayed there for a while and the same barman who'd been working the night before was there, so I asked – Has she been here? And he was like – (sharp intake of breathe) Ehh, no. And I was like – Hmmm. So after a while I realised – Alright already, she's not going to fucking turn up.

I'd had one joint left, which I'd rolled to smoke with her, and she had said that she lived around the corner from the bar, so I, like a gobshite, walked around looking to see if I'd accidentally bump into her. Of course I didn't. Slowly but surely I realised that I'd made a fool out of myself and it was time to move on. That was the end of it. So off I went to explore Paris alone. I smoked the joint. Man, she was stunning. She was from Germany actually, from Munich, and her name was Natalia.

I went to La Bastille and was surrounded by people all dressed up and out for the night. I couldn't feel bad about Natalia, because we'd had a nice evening and then I fucked it up by being weird – so I just had to be happy for the experience. And I was still just glad that I'd talked to her at all.

La Bastille had a big set of steps across from the statue near the river. At the top was a group of people hanging out. One guy was playing a strange instrument that looked like a big bow-and-arrow but sounded like a bass. Two chocolate-skinned French babes sung and rapped along. It was hypnotic. This was coolness on a previously unimaginable scale.

I felt that just being there at La Bastille in Paris, at that moment, was the "be-all-and-end-all"; the high point of my life so far. This was getting to be a daily occurrence. Lucky me. I buzzed all around the different bars and cafés, even having an Irish whiskey – just for the craic.

At one point I saw a load of Moroccan looking individuals acting shady. I marched into the middle of them and announced "Excusez moi, Je suis Irlandais, et Je recherche pour l'herb, s'il vous plaît."

This made them laugh, and before I knew it I was the proud owner of a fine chunk of Moroccan hashish. Lovely. I whipped a quick joint together in a toilet and bounced along through the crowds, savouring the surroundings.

All of a sudden a big black guy started walking alongside me, in my stride. Very strange. "Guillotine!" he said – "Guillotine" I laughed right back at him.

The laughter caught him off guard. Suddenly I realised that he'd probably wanted to physically confront me, but somehow the laughter had thrown him off. So I offered him the joint. He took it.

We were at the bottom of the steps where the people were jamming. We sat down and chatted away in French/English. He was in a bad way. He said he was on some legal drugs to wean him off heroin. I rolled another joint, not that it'd make much difference to him. It gave me something to do with my hands. The jammers jammed away. Both of us couldn't believe that I wasn't frightened, it seemed.

By all accounts I should've been scared. This guy might have had a weapon, and was off his head on fuck knows what. But having travelled all those countries in a row I was feeling invincible. And I was also going with the flow as never before. For his part he did calm down a bit from the spliffs. It didn't do any harm at least.

Towards the end he started getting freaky and going "I know who you are", meaning some sort of evil spirit or something. At this point I decided to head off. He protested a bit but then let me go, thank fuck. I gave him some hash, cigarettes and papers, then waved goodbye, high on hash and adrenalin.

After finding a hotel, I wrote my bollocks off. At this stage I was undoubtedly beginning to lose it. Sleep, travel, and sensory overload – it was all kicking in. I was living in a confused mind, and the impressions kept on coming.

The whole left-brain/right-brain thing really started getting out of hand in Paris. Walking down the streets I was ranting away internally with myself… "Fuck Off-ism" was supposed to be pronounced with a smile. It was basically a "let's-start-over/we're-all-as-full-of-shit-as-each-other" type of idea, and the way forward was to fuck right off.

It was all about going with the flow, giving people the benefit of the doubt, and staying open minded. It involved seeing with your third eye. I'd read about some guy who'd envisaged a cultural evolution. He reckoned people would eventually just start acting appropriately. Were things getting worse or better?

Bob Geldof was a Fuck Off-ist. Ghandi was a Fuck Off-ist. John Lydon, Mohammad Ali, and Emeline Pankhurst were all Fuck Off-ists in their own ways. Of course there was some tomfoolery in calling it "Fuck Off-ism", just to get up the nose of those folks who'd be offended by "the 'F' word". Feck them.

The left-brain/right-brain tête-à-tête went on unabated…

…Somebody once said that every generation
has to make its own discoveries -
even if they're old discoveries…
Maybe, just maybe, there's more
undiscovered than uncovered…

There was something to do with the search for truth about all of this. That had been the whole point of the journey, to search for what's real, for what isn't bullshit doled out to us by corrupt governments or soulless corporations. I was looking for some truth behind all the lies, if there even was any truth.

It was true I was finding it hard to cope with all the stuff that was going on in my head. The hardest part was not being able to write it down quickly enough. It felt essential to record these thoughts; Fuck off, get away, go somewhere you've never been before, alter your perspective, change your point of view – and (y)our point of you. That's where the truth lies. How can the truth lie?

20. San Sebastian

Mr. Eiffel, who did the tower in Paris, also designed the train station in San Sebastián. So there. To the people here it wasn't San Sebastián in Spain, it was Donosti in Euskada – the Basque Country. I'd got to know two lads from here that had lived in the Irish field in Amsterdam. They played mean guitar.

It was a gorgeous morning when I got into town. After meeting the lads we went to one of their apartments. I had to try to speak French with the lady of the house, who spoke Spanish or French. It was a very basic chat, with lots of nodding and smiling.

We buzzed off around the town. The lads showed me all the best places – it was a beautiful city. Having said that, we saw loads of graffiti about E.T.A. (the Basque Separatists). Some bars were festooned with flags and pictures of E.T.A. volunteers. It was really reminiscent of Northern Ireland – only sunnier and without the army presence. I didn't mention it. Anyway you couldn't shut me up about Fuck Off-ism.

The lads were hospitable as be jeasus, sorting out everything and taking pride in their beloved city. We sat on some steps up on a hill overlooking the bay – the Bay of Biscay – smoking some incredibly strong Ketama hashish, direct from Morocco. It was way stronger than what passed for Ketama in Amsterdam. The lads had said that that wasn't real Ketama. I could now understand their point entirely.

There'd been a bunch of us, a big community, on the campsite in Amsterdam. So far, I was the only one who had been lucky enough to visit them here, so it felt a bit like being an ambassador. They bought me tortilla. It was scrumptious.

After a big farewell with the lads in the train station, I only got a couple of stations away and then had to walk for ages to the next station. I came to a bridge and realised that I'd accidentally reached the border between Spain and France. The train station was on the French side.

On either side of the bridge were E.U. signs saying "France" and "España". But both had been spray-painted over with the word "Euskada". The Basque Country extends into France. Knackered, I sat down and noted…

...What is the fucking story with nationalities and territories and nationalism and terrorism?

It's fucked up.

At the station I'd hoped to get a train via Lyon towards Bamberg, but unfortunately the only option was to go via Paris. This meant it was going to take nearly twenty-four hours of train travel to get to Bamberg. What was worse – I'd only a few Pesetas left. Still, it was definitely worth visiting the lads in their part of the world.

21. Bamberg Again

The twenty-four hour journey from the south west corner of France was nuts. I had no food, no money and no ciggies. I asked strangers for cigarettes – the fellow-smoker-bond breaking down international barriers.

Having said that, it didn't always go down well, especially in one small German town. The man looked like I'd asked to sleep with his Granny. He still gave me a smoke though. On this leg of the journey I mulled things over in the notebook, questioning everything…

…Is it good enough to be good at what you do?
Shouldn't we try to be good at what we think?

It was lovely to be back in Bamberg again. This time the Bier Fest was on, and the town was packed with tourists. I turned up in a quivering mess – knackered and starving. After eating a quick meal we headed out to the festival.

Bamberg is a beautiful town and during the Bier Fest the streets are full of revellers revelling. This year there were four Dublin lads participating at full throttle.

Irish people at a German Bier Fest means mayhem, bedlam and chaos: boisterousness in general, piggyback races, break dancing, loud singing, laughing, wrestling and more. ("Sorry!")

Someone even tried to start a fight with one of the lads, who was a Northside Dubliner, so it was not a shrewd move and was quickly put to bed. "Don't even go there, pal". It was great being amongst the lads again. Being Irish can be a seriously good laugh. We partied our arses off.

Obviously I had everything to tell about what had happened since being in Bamberg the week before – the Amsterdam Mindfuck, Belgian Beer, Parisian Joie de Vivre, Basque Separatism and of course Fuck Off-ism.

The lads thought that Fuck Off-ism was "different", to say the least. They humoured me. I was unrelenting but harmless, mostly.

After discussing Fuck Off-ism with the lads at length, I was more charged up than ever. I told them what happened in Amsterdam with the whole "Putting-things-into-words" thing. They didn't know what to make of it, as I didn't. But it still felt good. It felt like I held undisclosed information about how great life actually is, and so I was eager to disclose it. Fair play to the lads, they indulged me, which was a big help.

22. Amsterdam Again II

My train from Bamberg continued northwards. Somewhere after Cologne the train split into two. The first half went to Brussels. The back, with a new engine, went to Amsterdam. I needed to be in the back but was in the front.

Had I been arsed I could've been very pissed off about this, but it was actually nice to be back in Brussels. It was fun to be surrounded by serious business people doing serious things, when I was just a travelling vagabond in between sessions. I had the shortest of looks around, just a tip of the cap, and then headed for Amsterdam. My head was still buzzing off the Bier Fest in Bamberg. I scribbled away…

...Sometimes I feel like I'm in the flow
and the only thing I'm aware of is the flow
and how unaware I am of the nature of it all.
All I'm aware of is my unawareness?
We can only describe the "unknown"
in terms of the "known", I suppose...

This time I was going to be arriving in and leaving Amsterdam on the same day. I got there and checked my bank account – I'd been paid my last few Guilders. "Holiday Pay" they called it. I liked the sound of that. Lovely jubbly.

On the train I'd met a guy from America. We ended up going for a game of Trick-shot Pool in the Hill Street Blues. The game got creative – the rules being that firstly, there were no rules, and secondly, that every shot had to be a trick shot. We ended up breaking some new ground. On the stereo was the Pink Floyd song where the end of it goes into the fans singing at Liverpool football club. It was most atmospheric.

After that I dropped into a big hotel where one of the Irish lasses worked. Eventually I found her in the staff canteen after sending security into a tizzy by trying to surprise her while she was cleaning the rooms – fuck the system!

The rest of the gang all met up and sessioned on down in downtown Amsterdam. A pleasurable time was had by all, even though most of what I had to say was unintelligible. I made the evening train, with various individuals sending me off on the platform. It was finally farewell ("Tot ziens!") to good old Amsterdam after a long crazy summer.

A tad partied-up at this stage, I got on the train, dumped my bag on a free seat and went back to the door to say my goodbyes to everyone. There was a jovial mood. As the train pulled away there was mass waving on both sides.

Smiling broadly, I went back to my seat. The bag was gone, with everyfuckingthing in it. Shit! I turned to the nearest passenger; "Did you see someone take a bag from here? No?"

Fuck. My heart was in my mouth and the bottom was falling out of my world. Man! What to do? I went walking up the train looking for somebody with my bag. I got to the next carriage. There was my bag, right where I'd left it on the seat. Phew! I laughed at myself and collapsed in a heap.

23. Paris Again

Usually after sessions in Amsterdam, you'll sleep quite soundly. I woke up on the train to Paris with an Alsatian dog sniffing at my face and a French Cop saying something in French. Freaky. They left and I went back to sleep. Waking up as we arrived in La Gare du Nord I felt tingles of excitement running through me – how jammy was I to be living this holiday? Being back in Paris made me feel sophisticated as fuck. This whole trip was going to my head. I thought I was only fucking "IT".

Paris was so unique. French people were very Fuck Off-ist (in a good way, that is). Another aspect to the Fuck Off-ism thing was seeing both sides of the coin, the big picture, and the middle way, as the Buddhists say. I got my fortune told by a fortune teller on the street. He verified that I was indeed "IT" (at least that's how I saw it), and said be careful.

The whole time I was walking around in a daze, in my own little movie, writing the script as I went along, loving every minute of it. Intuition was calling the shots.

France, the French, Français, I soaked it all up, feeling lucky, and on a mission, intoxicated with whatever the fuck was keeping me going. Somehow I had faith that I could communicate or explain all these feelings; seeing all these places, hearing the languages, touching the coins, tasting the foods, smelling the aromas…

At one point I asked someone the way, and they told me to follow the Seine, which sounded like "Follow the Sane". I knew I'd lost it but I didn't care. I was still alive, and free. I just couldn't get enough of hanging out in cafés in Paris.

I met up with one of the lads who was living in Paris but had been away when I'd been there before. We went to Père Lachaise Cemetery where Oscar Wilde is buried, and Jim Morrison, and lots of other important dead folk.

It was the most incredible graveyard I'd ever been in. Lots of very rich dead people, who evidently tried to take it with them, or at least decorate their grave as much as possible. One of the books that I'd had with me while travelling around was *The Sayings of Oscar Wilde*. So at his graveside I wrote a note…

Nobody described the paradox of life like he did,
and here he is, dead - in the earth with the rest.
If life's only certainty is death, let's live it up..!

I explained Fuck Off-ism to my friend. He also indulged me. People generally didn't know how to react to Fuck Off-ism. This tended to make me try to explain it all more clearly. "Y' know, Fuck Off-ism – what the world's been waiting for, the solution to what's wrong with everything…"

My friend had never come across somebody this convinced of themselves, yet clearly off their rocker. He later said it was both amusing and bemusing, fun yet nuts.

24. London

NO SKINS
HEAD
NO PROB-
LEM

The boat journey from France was really rough. I, like most people, spent the whole of the crossing trying not to puke. At last I was finally back in an English speaking country; England, no less.

London was another sort of homecoming. Four years previously, having worked the summer in London, I'd hoped to go inter-railing but it hadn't work out. This was a triumphant return. I paraded around Marble Arch and up Oxford Street to Tottenham Court Road. I'd done it by George. Jolly Good. Tea, anyone?

This time I'd been all over Europe in a flash, and now had Fuck Off-ism to share with the world – for better or worse. Since being here in May I'd seen so much it was fucked up, but what I'd lived in the last month was *fucking* fucked up.

One of the lasses from Ireland was living in South London. We met up and partied like good things. I lovingly explained the whole Fuck Off-ism thing to her.

Again there was some humouring and indulgence, but this time with more disbelief, laughter and even sympathy – like "Fuck Off-ism? Oh, right, okay, good luck with that then…"

There was no stopping it though – Fuck Off-ism it was. Fucking off here there and everywhere. I had notebooked…

Fuck Off-ism: not giving a fuck - in a positive way, while not fucking anybody else up. In other words, being fully open to new thoughts, impressions and ideas - from the point of view that what we know is so small compared to what there is to know.

Everything that there was to be seen, heard, and smelt had an implication for Fuck Off-ism. Punks? Fuck Off-ist music fans. Cockney Rhyming Slang? A Fuck Off-ist means of communication. Whiskey? A Fuck Off-ist drink, and so on and on and on…

We again Leicester Squared and Covent Gardened into the early hours. Splendid. Spiffing. You just couldn't beat London for multiculturalism, and for architecture, and pomp.

I reflected, what about the other cities that'd been centres of Empires? Vienna, Budapest, Berlin, and Paris all had lots of big architecture, lots of "don't-fuck-with-us" vibes. Yet all these Empires eventually crumbled. All those cities now have big "don't-fuck-with-us" corporate buildings, with corporate crime and corrupt conglomerates and all that lark. And that's only if we believe half of what we're led to think.

25. Edinburgh

The train to Edinburgh passed through Newcastle. These parts were the home of Jack Charlton, Saviour of Irish Football. We dashed past the Border; you could just make out the sign. Och aye, laddie, Bonnie Scotland! I didn't have a whole lot of money left and wasn't sure how much it'd be on the ferry back to Ireland. For the laugh I made a sign on a piece of cardboard – "Irishman in need of Scotch, please help!". I had a plan.

After arriving in Edinburgh I had a quick walk around to get my bearings. I picked a pretty crowded street, put down my bag, put the sign on the ground, got my balls out and started juggling. I juggled away and hoped someone would give me some money. No one did. I tried all the tricks I knew - one ball over the back of the head, kicking one ball with the side of the foot – the lot. No pennies. Not a dickie bird.

For a good forty-five minutes I stood there juggling. Out of sheer boredom I started singing as I juggled, making the words up as I went along. "Oh please wouldya give us a few bob for a wee dram. Step right up. Will anyone help a fellow Celt?" That sort of shite.

After about 40 minutes I was still there juggling, and now singing too, having made a grand total of 10p. A man came up and gave me a pound coin – a whole pound! I was so happy. I looked him in the eye and said "Wow, thanks!" very enthusiastically indeed. He whispered, "Well listen", looking over my shoulder and down the street, "I've got some hash if you wanna go smoke a joint." No sooner had he finished his sentence than the balls and sign were back in the bag, and we were on our way to the park in the middle of Edinburgh.

We smoked a joint. He was sound, Jake from England, lived on an island off the west coast of Scotland. We talked about travelling. He reckoned it should be mandatory. Everybody should have to do some travelling on their own.

He also advised against busking. He said from his experience you actually make more money just panhandling people. It was sad but true. You can entertain people and they'll accept it for free, but hassle them and they'll pay you to leave them alone.

He had to go and catch a bus, but he left me a substantial nodge of hash, plenty for the last leg of the journey. He was a gentleman and a scholar, one of many people who'd helped me along the way. I smiled after him. He was a Fuck Off-ist.

Having expected the obligatory Scottish rain, the weather was actually sunny. Off I buzzed all around Edinburgh's streets. There was something familiar about it. I was starting to look forward to going home. I found a nice hostel and relaxed. In the notebook another "fuck everything" rant came on…

...Fuck modern art, fuck all that pretension,
fuck that anal retention, fuck designer crap,
fuck the Emperor's new threads, fuck the Empire.

Isn't all this patriotism just a tad patronising..?*

There was a Swiss guy and an Aussie guy in the hostel room. We got talking. I'd bought a half-bottle of Scotch for four quid (when in Scotland, and all that…). We shared it and the hash and had a natter. I spared them Fuck Off-ism. We shared stories of our travels. It was good craic.

After a couple of hours I left the hostel and walked through the town. In one pub I was the only customer. So I chatted to the bar maid for the length of a beer, then went to another pub where I was the only person not with a crowd of people. Both opposites felt strange. I thought about the middle path between the two extremes… again…

Having walked the highly impressive Royal Mile, I sat on a wall to have a smoke and got talking to a guy on the street. It turned out he was a heroin addict.

He told me his story. I told him mine. He was going to have to rob someone that night for his fix. He'd find someone easier than me to rob, he said. I wasn't convinced but stayed talking with him. We had a good chat. The difference between his situation and mine was unreal. He said something that stuck in my mind. His father died of addiction to alcohol, and he'd die of addiction to heroin. Same difference, he reckoned.

Back in the hostel I lay in bed and deliberated long and hard about "IT" (that was the word that I thought made the most sense to describe it – "IT"). I was back to contemplating the unknown. Having come from a fascistly Catholic island, the idea of "God" was stomach-turning for me. But was spirituality, as opposed to religion, altogether unthinkable?

Could it be that I'd experienced some kind of "enlightenment" in Amsterdam with the "putting-things-into-words" incident? Or was it an awakening? Either way it sure was unorthodox. An atheist was supposed to be somebody who didn't believe in "God" whatsoever. And an agnostic was apparently someone who believed that nothing is known, or likely to be known, of the existence of "God".

I definitely reckoned there was hope of knowing more about the unknown – learning more about the unlearnt. But the whole "God fearing worship" thing conjured up the wrong image. It implied something outside or above or beyond us. Whereas, whatever the fuck that it was, it was in us, within us. We were it. It was us.

26. Glasgow

It was a wonderful wee journey across Scotland. I got into Glasgow and looked around. It was pretty hilly. I was running out of tourist energy. I checked out the centre a bit and saw a sign that said "Give Blood". Okay then. In I went and signed the form, sat down and chatted away with the friendly Glaswegian women.

Their accents were great. I was all ready to give the blood when the nurse said to me "You haven't had a cold lately or anything have you, love?" I realised that I'd had a bit of a sniffle. She said we'd better not chance it. I still got the free tea and biscuits that blood donors got. The ladies were great. Glasgow Celtic supporters one and all – loved the Irish to bits.

By this stage I was actually beginning to feel grateful that the whole journey was coming to an end. I was tired, but inspired. Was I going to create some mad imaginative stuff with the contents of my head? I was oblivious to the idea that people might not understand what I was on about. I wrote away in the notebook as if everyone in the world would catch my drift…

...What's that?

Consciously co-operating with IT

Beneficial mutualITy
And mutual benefIT
And HumilITy
BefITting IT...

Glasgow was so much like home that I wished I was home. All the same, it was great to be in Billy Connolly's hometown - one of the funniest men alive. For the laugh I sent a postcard to Jake on his Island to say thanks again. Where would you be without friendly strangers who treated you like a guest?

27. Liverpool

Live it up
in Liverpool
BEATLES
Story
For details of big savings on days and nights by train, pick up a leaflet
14 AUGUST 1995 - 30 JUNE 1996
REGIONAL RAILWAYS

They call Liverpool the Irish capital of England, which sounds a bit Irish really. I'd been a supporter of Liverpool football club since I was a kid, and of course I loved the Beatles, so being in Liverpool was totally orgasmic. It was just a shame this was such a flying visit, it would've been cool to see Anfield. Ah well, next time…

Still, I loved it, moseyin' around Merseyside. It definitely was beginning to feel more and more like home. Ireland was just across that stretch of water. Wow, I'd seen the Baltic Sea, the River Danube, the River Inn, the Adriatic, and the Bay of Biscay. Just one more body of water and I'd be home.

With the Beatles on my headphones I walked around and round. So this is where they hung out? It was very like Dublin really; rough and raw. I remembered the Pink Floyd song in Amsterdam with all the Liverpool fans singing at the end – "You'll Never Walk Alone". I was walking alone, but on air…

I sat down on the steps of some church and had a smoke. A group of laughing Liverpudlians were heading out for the night, all rowdy and happy. They could have easily been a crowd of Dubliners. The Beatles came from Liverpool so it'll always be cool. But it doesn't matter if you're from Timbuktu – it's not where you're from it's where you're @. Notebook…

…There's nothing U can think that can't be thunk,
Nothing U can sink that can't be sunk (thank fuck)
Nothing you can B that isn't what you're meant 2B

IT's easy… all you need - is to fuck off…

There was an edginess on the streets of Liverpool that was familiar from Dublin. It was different to mainland Europe. The possibility of violence was in the air the whole time.

28. Holyhead

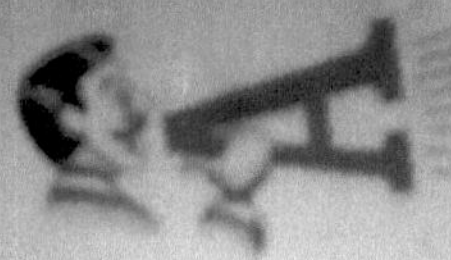

COMMUNIC[illegible] BY DESIGN '95

On the way from Liverpool to Holyhead there was a weirdo on the train. He was talking to himself as well as the other passengers. They ignored him. I, like an idiot, talked back to him. Within minutes I was his best friend.

In between rants, he took it upon himself to teach me how to pronounce the longest place name in Wales. It took a while – and along the way he showed his just-escaped-from-an-asylum tendencies. But after lots of effort he got me to say the word 'Llanfairpwllgwyngyllgogerychwyrndrobwllllantysiliogogogoch'.

He got off the train before Holyhead, thankfully. A lady nearby smiled at me. She was glad the weirdo had stayed away from her. The poor bloke was just confused, off his head on prescription drugs. Still, it was actually fun in a childlike way. Sure we're all a bit mad, I suppose. Random notebook entry…

...People may say - "Oh, you think you're IT"
Eye'd say yeah, eye do, eye know eye'm "IT"...
Why don't you...?

Why don't you just switch off your television set and go out and do something less boring instead?
"Could you be loved?" Only if you love yourself.
Don't ya gotta love the shit out of (y)ourself..?

I was definitely loving the shit out of myself, no doubt about it. Reaching Holyhead felt like I'd just run a marathon. In my head there were lots of different characters patting me on the back. I'd done it, I'd fucking done it! This was the final part of the trip. I got on board and walked all over the boat. It was the same one as in May when Ajax had won the Champions League. That seemed like a lifetime ago.

Man, I'd seen so much since then. Was it too much to handle? I felt not, purely because I'd survived it. But the quantity and quality of impressions and ideas along the way were just ridiculous – talk about the University of Life.

Back in Ireland people were going to ask how the trip was. What was I going to do, break into hysterical laughter? Describing the sights, sounds, smells, and tastes wouldn't be so hard. Describing the thoughts and ideas could only really be hinted at. But at this stage I was sure that everybody would "get" Fuck Off-ism. Either way the wind was in the sails.

29. Dun Laoghaire

This time the boat crossing was as smooth as a baby's arse. I was thrilled skinny to be arriving back in Dun Laoghaire. Finally this was the real homecoming. The coastline came into view through the window. My heart jumped and I rushed out on deck. The sky was grey and it was drizzling. Classic Ireland.

You could see Killiney Hill, the Dublin Mountains, Howth, fishing boats, yachts, and the train line – home. I felt "blessed" somehow that I'd managed to get back in one piece (if the boat didn't sink between here and the harbour).

If anything was going to bring me back down to earth it would be some Dublin wit. "Taking the piss" was an art form in Ireland, and nobody was exempt. I was looking forward to being brought down a peg or two. My head was pretty much up my arse at this stage. I knew I was maybe a bit out of it – in that I wasn't "normal". I felt abnormal, but also unabashed and invigorated.

Nobody had experienced what I had, so I felt like nobody had the right to judge me. That couldn't last very long in Dublin. They'd be taking the piss to new heights.

I couldn't believe that I hadn't got laid somewhere along the line. Then again, thinking about it, I couldn't believe that I couldn't believe that. What was I like? I thought about Natlia. I fucked that one up. Ah well, you've got to laugh really.

Some home truths were needed. I flicked through the notebook. It was full of the words "Fuck Off-ism". Quite. It also had lots of references to "IT", but I hadn't really captured the meaning of "IT". Out it churned into the notebook all the same…

… Are we blissfully unaware of the process that we are a part of, individually and collectively…?

Yeah, yeah, yeah. Anyway, the voyage was nearly over now. The boat glided into Dun Laoghaire harbour. It was about nine in the morning, and the people of little old Ireland's capital were just beginning to nurse their hangovers. I knew this place like no other.

But now it was going to be different. What I'd experienced had changed me. I had found some sort of truth that was contrary to the perceived wisdom, and felt compelled to tell people about IT. Fucking off was to be highly recommended, as was telling people who needed to be told to fuck off, to fuck off. Also important was being able to look at yourself in the mirror and tell yourself to fuck off, while smiling. I made one last entry in the notebook …

...What can U do when U can't change something
only change the way that U are looking @ IT
SomewHERE inside there is some strength
that helps your head with that shhhh...IT

And either way, at the end of the day,
U are always (y)our own best friend...

Somehow IT all* seems
to work out in
the end.

"(*Not all, just most, so enough)" – this was another phrase that was all over the notebook. Brendan Behan, who'd looked over my shoulder back in Berlin, described returning by boat to Ireland in his book *The Borstal Boy*. Fucking hell, I thought, our lives are so easy compared to people like him.

And what about the Welsh weirdo, the smackhead in Edinburgh, the guillotine guy in Paris, and all the victims in Auschwitz? You just have to make the most of your luck…

The boat docked and I stepped back onto Irish soil at last. I could've kissed the ground, but this was Dublin, someone might have pissed on it the night before. So I just smiled and strolled on up the road into Dun Laoghaire. Home.

30. Epilogue

NO
YES
HATE
LOVE DAY
NIGHT LIFE
DEATH MAN
WOMAN OLD
YOUNG FAT THIN
HOLY EVIL CLEVER
STUPID RICH POOR SICK
HEALTHY BLACK WHITE
BIG SMALL HAPPY SAD LAND
SEA WATER FIRE SQUARE ROUND
NORTH SOUTH EAST WEST LEFT
RIGHT BACK FORTH THEM US IN OUT
SUPPLY DEMAND SHIT FOOD
UP DOWN WAR PEACE MAD
SANE AWAKE ASLEEP HELLO
GOODBYE THANKS PLEASE
ALL NOTHING START
AND END?

YIN
YANG

The few months after the trip were insane. Needless to say I freaked everyone out with Fuck Off-ism. Bewilderment was the general reaction. Luckily that time doesn't have to be lived through again. I kept misquoting people, thinking I was "IT". Loved ones worried. Friends cringed. Grown men grimaced.

All I can tell you is that I lived to tell this tale, and it was a lively tale to live. The only thing I could do was write and write and rewrite and so on and on…

After nit picking the shit out of it, the "Why Not" book was finally completed. It only took seven years, in a few different countries, with plenty of ups and downs, and middles and riddles and fiddles and violins and trumpets… and the like. Still, these things are better off the chest.

On the trip I saw things I'd never seen and did things I'd never done. But/yet/and in actual fact that happens all the time. You do learn something new everyday. There was something to learn on each of those thirty-one days, and every day since. Anyway, I've learnt enough to know that I've got a lot to learn.

Looking at the big picture, that whole journey barely amounted to a cursory glance around. This story has been written as a letter for my lover, explaining the craziest trip I've ever had (so far). Maybe it's also a half-arsed apology to the people whose heads I wrecked. But sure it's all water under the bridge now – a bridge over troubled waters…

These days I try to be as open-minded as I like to think I am. To be honest, I still don't really know what happened to me that time in Amsterdam with the "Putting-things-into-words" thing. It has me in awe to this day. I accidentally tripped a switch somewhere inside my head, some inner voice, presumably. Something like that. I don't know. At the end of the day it's just a moment in time from another point of view. That's "IT". Yes.

www.ingramcontent.com/pod-product-compliance
Ingram Content Group UK Ltd.
Pitfield, Milton Keynes, MK11 3LW, UK
UKHW041941190726
13854UKWH00004B/1732

9 781847 994349